To the SUPER Marion and all my SUPER dear friends at Leigh Writers,
with much love and thanks for all your encouragement
and support over the years.
C.F.

For Stuart,
who has stronger superpowers of patience
and kindness than anyone I've ever met.
S.M.

This edition published in 2019
First published in 2013 by Scholastic Children's Books
Euston House, 24 Eversholt Street
London NW1 1DB
a division of Scholastic Ltd
www.scholastic.co.uk
London – New York – Toronto – Sydney – Auckland
Mexico City – New Delhi – Hong Kong

Text copyright © 2013 Claire Freedman
Illustrations copyright © 2013 Sarah McIntyre
PB ISBN 978 1407 188 75 1

SUPERKID

Written by Claire Freedman

Illustrated by Sarah McIntyre

SCHOLASTIC

There's a boy who seems quite ordinary,
He looks like me or you,

SUPERKID

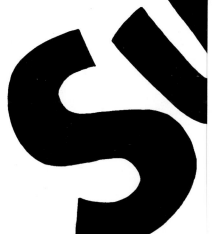

CLAIRE FREEDMAN

SARAH McINTYRE

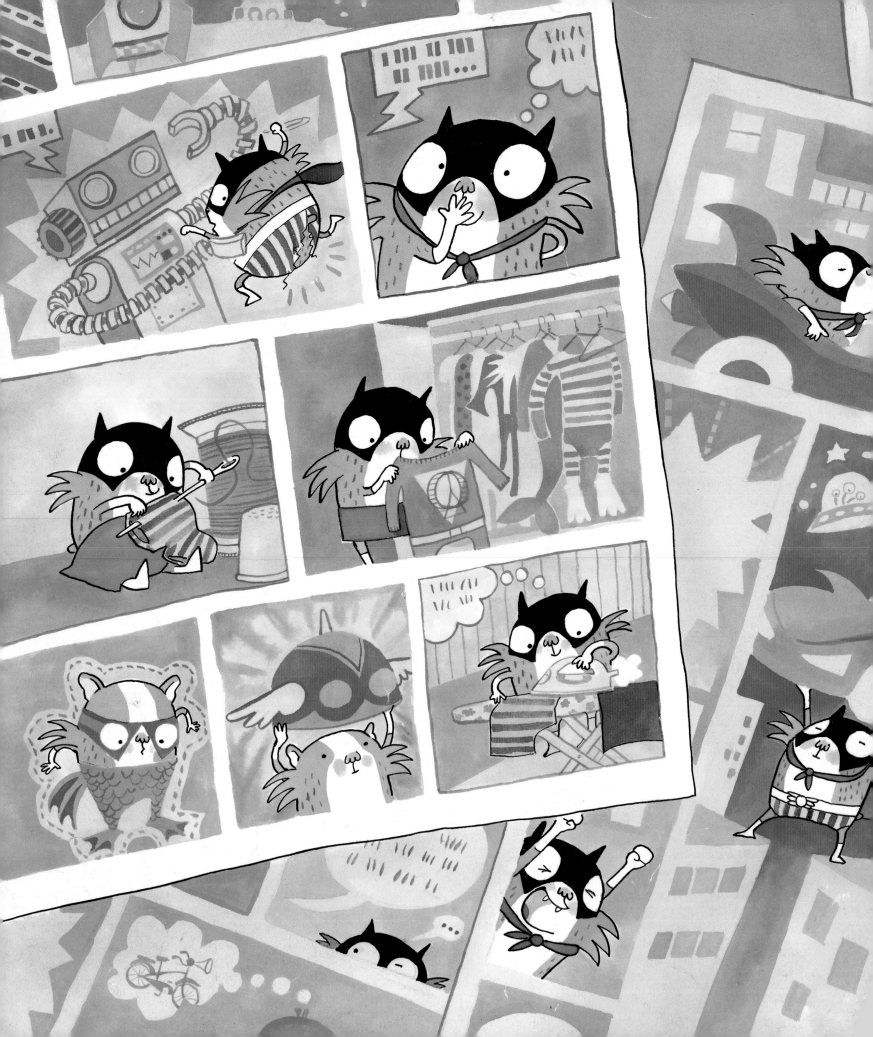

But in secret…
he is

SUPERKID!

There's nothing
he can't do!

Behind his glasses

X-RAY EYES

Can spot a child
in trouble.

Then, WHEEEE!

He changes
in a flash...

To help them –
at the double!

If bullies pinch your bubble gum
As you go out to play,

WHOOSH!

Superkid
comes flying...

Yes! He's here
to save the day.

He blows a giant bubble
And the kids stick to its side.
Then

PuFF!

He blows it in the air,
And off those bullies ride!

When you're having tea at Auntie's,
But it's all the food you hate,

And Auntie says,
"More broccoli?"

And
piles
it
on
your
plate…

ZAPPP!

Superkid comes whizzing,

And before your Auntie sees…

He eats the
dreaded broccoli…
And horrid
mushy peas!

There's a great film on one evening
That you really must not miss…

But your mum says, "No more watching 'til you've tidied all of this!"

Poor Mum is almost fainting,
"Surely this can't be YOUR room!"

But what if you're out with a friend
And meet a pirate crew...

Who say, "We're on a treasure hunt,
There's room on board for you!"

But then they make you walk the plank.

Yikes!
In the churning sea...

...Swim hungry snapping sharks that laugh,

"We'll
eat
you
for our tea!"

He rescues
you, then **THWACK!**

He sorts those
evil pirates out,
And flies you
safely back!

So when you're with your friends at school,
Watch carefully what they do.

You might just find that

SUPERKID

Is sitting next to...

YOU!